caillou ®

Puts Away his Toys

A Chouette Publishing adaptation
Original text by Joceline Sanschagrin, based on the animated series
Illustrations: CINAR Animation

chouette CINAR

Caillou had made a big
mountain out of his toys and
was hiding underneath.
"Caillou, where are you?"
his mommy called out.
"Too bad Caillou has
disappeared," she said.
"He won't get any
chocolate pudding."
Caillou loved chocolate
pudding.
"Wait for me, Mommy!"

"Look at this mess! What did I tell you, Caillou?"
"I'm not supposed to leave my toys on the stairs,"
he replied.
"Go and put them away, please!"

With his arms full of toys, Caillou went back upstairs. When Caillou went into the kitchen, Rosie was already there, eating her chocolate pudding.

"Caillou!" called Daddy.
"Come here, please."
"You'd better go and see
what Daddy wants," said
Mommy.
Slowly, Caillou put down
his spoon.

"Caillou, what have
I told you about
leaving your toys all
over the driveway?"
"I'm supposed to
put away my toys,"
he replied.
"That's right!"

"But I haven't had my chocolate pudding yet!"
"Your pudding can wait," Daddy replied.
Unhappily, Caillou picked up his toys.
Daddy helped.
Caillou ran back to the kitchen. But Daddy called him again:
"Caillou, I'd like a word with you, in the bathroom."
"Uh-oh!" Caillou said.

"Caillou, you have to clean up your toys. Then you can have some pudding."
Caillou picked up his toys. "Phew!" said Caillou when he had finished.
"Are you sure you picked up *all* your toys?"

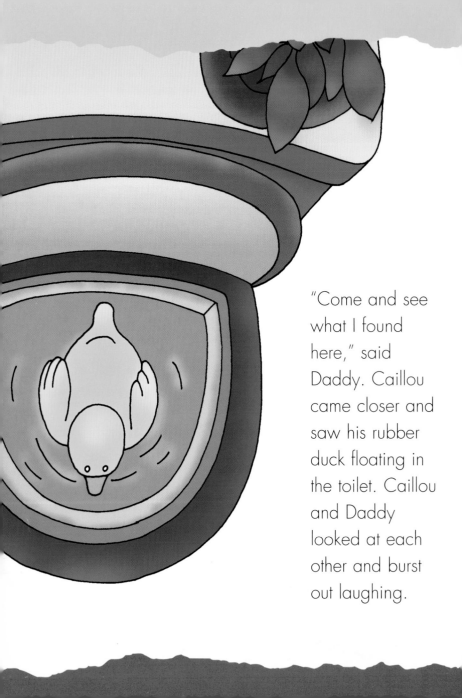

"Come and see what I found here," said Daddy. Caillou came closer and saw his rubber duck floating in the toilet. Caillou and Daddy looked at each other and burst out laughing.

At last! Caillou was eating his chocolate pudding.
"Caillou, you have so many toys!" Mommy said.
"There are a lot of toys you don't even play
with any more. What should we do with them?"
Daddy asked.
"You could give some to your sister," Mommy
suggested.
But Caillou loved
all his toys.
"I'll give one toy
to Rosie now
and maybe some
more later!"

Daddy had an idea. "Caillou, you need a big box for all your toys. I'll make one. Would you like to help me?"

"Oh, yes!" Caillou replied. "As soon as I finish my chocolate pudding."

Caillou was excited to be working with Daddy.
Both of them worked very hard. Caillou
held the nails and handed them to Daddy when
he needed them.
"Look, Caillou, now your toys have a
beautiful home."
"Thank you, Daddy!"

A Chouette Publishing adaptation of the original text by Joceline Sanschagrin, based on the
CAILLOU animated film series produced by CINAR Corporation (© 1997 Caillou Productions
Inc., a subsidiary of CINAR Corporation). All rights reserved.
Original scenario written by Matthew Cope.
Illustrations taken from the television series CAILLOU.
Graphic design: Monique Dupras
Computer graphics: Les Studios de la Souris Mécanique

Canadian Cataloguing in Publication Data

Sanschagrin, Joceline, 1950-
Caillou puts away his toys
New rev. ed.
(Backpack Series)
Translation of: Caillou range ses jouets
Previously published as: Caillou tidies his toys
For children aged 3 and up.
Co-published by: CINAR Corporation.

ISBN 2-89450-356-3

1. Storage in the home – Juvenile literature.   2. Toys – Juvenile literature.
3. Discipline of children – Juvenile literature.   I. CINAR Corporation.   II. Title
III. Title: Caillou tidies his toys.   IV. Series.

TX309.S2613 2002   j648'.8   C2002-941169-6

Legal deposit: 2002

We gratefully acknowledge the financial support of BPIDP and SODEC
for our publishing activities.

Printed in China
10 9 8 7 6 5 4 3 2 1